Library of Congress Cataloging-in-Publication Control Number: 2014030747
ISBN 978-0-545-47083-4

10 9 8 7 6 5 4 3 2 1   15 16 17 18 19
Printed in Malaysia 108   First edition, August 2015

The text and display type was set in Century Gothic. Book design by Elisha Cooper, David Saylor, and Charles Kreloff

8

AN ANIMAL ALPHABET

ELISHA COOPER

ORCHARD BOOKS • NEW YORK

AN IMPRINT OF SCHOLASTIC INC.

FIND THE 8*

FIND THE ONE ANIMAL ON EACH PAGE THAT
IS PICTURED 8 TIMES — 8 ANTS, 8 BADGERS,
8 CHICKENS. FIND ALL THE OTHER ANIMALS, TOO.
SOME MAY BE FAMILIAR, SUCH AS A CAT, AND
SOME NOT, SUCH AS A MUSKRAT. (FOR HELP, SEE
THE "DID YOU KNOW?" SECTION IN THE BACK.)
BUT EVERY ANIMAL IS AMAZING AND BEAUTIFUL
IN ITS OWN WAY. ESPECIALLY THE HIPPOPOTAMUS.
LET THE EXPLORING BEGIN!

*WHY THE NUMBER 8? BECAUSE 8 IS GREAT. BECAUSE 8 IS ROUND
AND ADORABLE. BECAUSE 8 IS FUN TO COUNT TO (MOVE OVER, 10).
BECAUSE 8 IS NOT TOO BIG, AND NOT SO SMALL, BUT JUST RIGHT.
BECAUSE 8 IS MY FAVORITE NUMBER.

AARDVARK, ABALONE, ALBATROSS, ALLIGATOR, ALPACA, ANT, ANTEATER, ANTELOPE, ARMADILLO

Bb

BADGER, BEAR, BEAVER, BISON, BOAR, BOBCAT, BOOBY, BUMBLEBEE, BUTTERFLY

CAMEL, CAT, CATERPILLAR, CHAMELEON, CHEETAH, CHICKEN, CHIMPANZEE, CHIPMUNK,
CICADA, CLAM, COCKROACH, COW, COYOTE, CRAB

Dd

DEER, DOG, DOLPHIN, DONKEY, DRAGONFLY, DUCK, DUNG BEETLE

EAGLE, EARTHWORM, EGRET, ELEPHANT, ELEPHANT SEAL, ELK

Ff

FALCON, FERRET, FIREFLY, FLAMINGO, FLYING SQUIRREL, FOX, FROG

GAZELLE, GERBIL, GIBBON, GIRAFFE, GNAT, GOAT, GOOSE, GOPHER, GORILLA,
GRASSHOPPER, GROUNDHOG, GUINEA PIG

Hh

HAMSTER, HAWK, HEDGEHOG, HERON, HIPPOPOTAMUS, HORSE, HUMMINGBIRD, HYENA

IBEX, IBIS, IGUANA, IMPALA, INCHWORM

Jj

JACKAL, JACKRABBIT, JAGUAR, JELLYFISH

KAKAPO, KANGAROO, KINGFISHER, KIWI, KOALA, KUDU

LADYBUG, LEMMING, LEMUR, LEOPARD, LION, LIZARD, LLAMA, LOON

Mm

MOLE, MONGOOSE, MOOSE, MOSQUITO, MOTH, MOUSE, MUSKRAT

Nn

NAKED MOLE RAT, NARWHAL, NEWT

OCTOPUS, ORCA, OSPREY, OSTRICH, OTTER, OWL, OYSTER

PANDA, PARROT, PELICAN, PENGUIN, PHEASANT, PIG, PIGEON, PLATYPUS, PORCUPINE, POSSUM, PUFFIN

QUAIL, QUETZAL, QUOLL

RABBIT, RACCOON, RAT, RAVEN, RHINOCEROS, ROADRUNNER

SALMON, SANDPIPER, SEAGULL, SEA HORSE, SEAL, SEA TURTLE, SHARK, SHEEP, SKUNK, SLOTH,
SLUG, SNAIL, SQUID, SQUIRREL, STARFISH, SWALLOW, SWAN, SWORDFISH

Tt

TARANTULA, TICK, TIGER, TOAD, TROUT, TUNA, TURKEY, TURTLE

Uu

UAKARI, UMBRELLA BIRD, UPUPA, URCHIN

Vv

VAMPIRE BAT, VIPER, VOLE, VULTURE

WALRUS, WARTHOG, WASP, WEASEL, WHALE, WOLF, WOLVERINE, WOMBAT

Xx

XERUS

YABBY, YAK, YAPOK, YELLOW JACKET

ZEBRA, ZEBRA DOVE, ZEBRA FINCH, ZEBRA FISH, ZEBU

THE END*

*BUT WAIT, THERE'S MORE! TURN THE PAGE.

Did you know?

 AARDVARK
Aardvarks are sometimes known as "ant bears."

 ABALONE
Abalone eat algae.

 **ALBATROSS**
The wide wingspan of the albatross lets it glide on wind currents for hours without flapping.

 ALLIGATOR
Newborn alligators ride inside their mother's mouth for safety.

 ALPACA
Alpacas hum when they are content.

 ANT
Most ants are female.

 ANTEATER
An anteater's tongue can be more than two feet long.

ANTELOPE
Antelope babies are able to walk minutes after they are born.

 **ARMADILLO**
Armadillos spend almost eighteen hours a day napping.

BADGER
Some badgers live in communal burrows, with separate compartments for eating and sleeping.

BEAR
Bears are bowlegged, which gives them better balance.

 BEAVER
Beavers can see underwater through transparent eyelids.

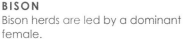 **BISON**
Bison herds are led by a dominant female.

 BOAR
Boars can smell food that is underground.

 BOBCAT
Bobcats are named for their short, "bobbed" tails.

 BOOBY
The male blue-footed booby has brighter blue feet than the female.

 BUMBLEBEE
Bumblebees shiver to warm up their flying muscles.

 **BUTTERFLY**
Butterflies taste with their feet.

 **CAMEL**
Camel humps store fat, not water.

 CAT
Cats purr when they are happy; they also purr when they are distressed.

 CATERPILLAR
Caterpillars have twelve eyes, but poor eyesight.

 CHAMELEON
A chameleon's eyes can look in different directions at the same time.

 CHEETAH
Cheetahs accelerate from zero to sixty miles per hour in three seconds, but overheat quickly and must slow down.

 CHICKEN
Chickens' eggs can be white, brown, blue, or green.

CHIMPANZEE
Chimpanzees are able to use tools, like twigs for spearing termites or leaves for collecting rainwater.

 CHIPMUNK
Chipmunks carry food in fur-lined cheek pouches.

 CICADA
Cicadas vibrate their stomach muscles to make a grating sound, which can be heard a mile away.

 CLAM
The oldest recorded age for a clam is over five hundred years.

 COCKROACH
Cockroaches can survive up to six weeks without eating.

 **COW**
Cows have four compartments in their stomachs, which help them eat hard-to-digest grass.

 COYOTE
To sneak up on prey, coyotes walk on their tiptoes.

 CRAB
Crabs can communicate by drumming and waving their claws.

 DEER
Deer can see blue, yellow, and green, but not orange or red.

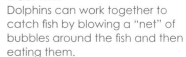 **DOG**
Dogs can sniff seven times a second.

DOLPHIN
Dolphins can work together to catch fish by blowing a "net" of bubbles around the fish and then eating them.

 DONKEY
A donkey's bray can last twenty seconds.

 DRAGONFLY
Dragonflies are able to see in almost all directions at once.

 DUCK
Ducks that eat food with their fronts in the water and their rears in the air are called "dabblers."

 DUNG BEETLE
Dung beetles are able to tell which direction they are going from the position of the sun and the stars.

 EAGLE
An eagle's nest can weigh more than two thousand pounds.

EARTHWORM
Bristly hairs on the earthworm's body help it move.

EGRET
Egrets will perch on top of elephants, hippopotamuses, and even alligators.

ELEPHANT
Elephants can flap their ears to communicate emotions to other elephants.

ELEPHANT SEAL
Elephant seals can hold their breath underwater for one hundred minutes.

ELK
Elk antlers grow about an inch a day during the summer.

FALCON
When hunting, falcons dive at speeds of two hundred miles per hour.

FERRET
A group of ferrets is called a "business."

FIREFLY
In many species of firefly, only the male firefly flies.

FLAMINGO
Flamingos are born with white or gray feathers, which turn pink from a diet of shellfish.

FLYING SQUIRREL
The flying squirrel can fly (glide, really) a hundred feet through the air.

FOX
Foxes use their tails for balance when they run; when cold, they wrap their tails around themselves for warmth.

FROG
Frogs can breathe through their skin.

GAZELLE
When gazelles run they sometimes bound in the air with all four hooves off the ground, a display called "pronking."

GERBIL
Gerbils have tails that can be shed if grabbed by a predator.

GIBBON
Gibbon couples start each day by hooting at each other.

GIRAFFE
The tongue of the giraffe is dark purple, which protects it from sunburn.

GNAT
An evening swarm of male gnats is called a "ghost."

GOAT
Some goats can climb trees.

GOOSE
When geese fly in a V formation it's called a "wedge."

GOPHER
Gophers use their tails to feel their way when crawling backward through a tunnel.

GORILLA
Gorillas yawn when they are nervous.

GRASSHOPPER
A grasshopper can jump twenty times the length of its body.

GROUNDHOG
Groundhogs sleep for most of the winter.

GUINEA PIG
When excited, guinea pigs hop.

HAMSTER
Hamsters will hunt insects in packs.

HAWK
Female hawks are often larger than male hawks.

HEDGEHOG
To protect themselves, hedgehogs roll into a ball with their spines pointing out.

HERON
Herons will eat mice.

HIPPOPOTAMUS
Hippopotamuses give birth in the water.

HORSE
Horses can sleep standing up.

HUMMINGBIRD
Hummingbirds can fly backward.

HYENA
The front legs of hyenas are longer than their back legs.

IBEX
The ibex's hoof has a hard edge and a soft center, which allows it to grip rocky terrain.

IBIS
Breeding ibis will wrap their necks around each other to show affection.

IGUANA
To defend themselves, iguanas will use their tails as weapons.

IMPALA
When impalas sense danger they bark at one another.

INCHWORM
Inchworms are actually not worms, but caterpillars that eventually become moths.

JACKAL
Jackal mothers move their pups to a new den every few weeks to keep them hidden.

JACKRABBIT
Jackrabbits' large ears help them keep cool by lowering the temperature of the blood that runs through them.

JAGUAR
Jaguars are excellent swimmers.

JELLYFISH
A jellyfish has no brain.

KAKAPO
Kakapos can't fly; they use their wings to parachute to the ground when jumping out of trees.

KANGAROO
Kangaroos can leap high in the air, but they can't walk backward.

KINGFISHER
Male and female kingfishers take turns sitting on their eggs.

KIWI
Kiwis' eggs are almost as large as their bodies.

KOALA
Koalas get their water from the leaves of eucalyptus trees.

KUDU
The male kudu's curvy horns grow up to six feet long.

LADYBUG
Ladybugs are sometimes known as "ladybirds" or "lady cows."

LEMMING
Lemmings build nests with grass and musk ox fur.

LEMUR
Lemurs enjoy sunbathing.

LEOPARD
Leopards hoard their prey high in trees to keep other animals from stealing it.

LION
The roar of a lion can be heard five miles away.

LIZARD
Lizards smell with their tongues.

LLAMA
Llamas stick out their tongues when they are angry.

LOON
Young loons sometimes ride on their parents' backs.

MOLE
A mole can eat fifty pounds of worms in a year.

MONGOOSE

Mongooses eat snakes, birds, lizards, insects, fruit, and eggs.

MOOSE

Moose's antlers amplify sound, helping them hear better.

MOSQUITO

Only female mosquitoes bite.

MOTH

Some moths have evolved to look unappetizing, mimicking wasps or bird poop.

MOUSE

Mice use their whiskers to gauge changes in the temperature.

MUSKRAT

Muskrats are able to swim both forward and backward.

NAKED MOLE RAT

Naked mole rats live in colonies where only the female "queen" reproduces.

NARWHAL

The tusk of the narwhal is actually one enlarged tooth.

NEWT

Newts can regenerate parts of themselves, including limbs, heart, and eyes.

OCTOPUS

Octopuses have three hearts.

ORCA

Orcas can land themselves on beaches in order to catch seals.

OSPREY

To catch fish, ospreys dive straight into the water from heights over a hundred feet.

OSTRICH

Ostriches have only two toes on each foot.

OTTER

A group of sea otters is called a "raft."

OWL
Owls have feathers that muffle the sound of their flight, allowing them to swoop silently down on prey.

OYSTER
A single oyster filters over forty gallons of water a day, cleaning water for other animal life.

PANDA
Pandas have an extra digit on their paws that helps them tear and eat bamboo.

PARROT

A parrot's beak keeps growing throughout its lifetime.

PELICAN

Pelicans have the largest bill of any bird.

PENGUIN

Penguins slide on their stomachs over ice and snow, which helps them save energy.

PHEASANT

Some male pheasants have a white ring around their necks.

PIG

Pigs can't sweat; they lie in mud to keep cool.

PIGEON

Pigeons are able to fly seven hundred miles in one day.

PLATYPUS

The male platypus has poisonous spurs on its back feet.

PORCUPINE

A threatened porcupine chatters its teeth and scurries backward.

POSSUM

Possums have tails that help them grasp and climb trees.

PUFFIN

Puffins sometimes build nests in old rabbit burrows.

QUAIL

To fool predators, quails lie on their sides and play dead.

QUETZAL

The tail feathers of the male quetzal can be twice as long as its body.

QUOLL

Quolls use communal toilet areas.

RABBIT

When chased, rabbits run in a zigzag pattern.

RACCOON

Raccoons rinse their food before eating it.

RAT
Rats can tread water for three days.

RAVEN
Ravens are playful, and will use sticks as toys.

RHINOCEROS
The skin of the rhinoceros is more than an inch thick.

ROADRUNNER

Roadrunners prefer walking and running to flying.

SALMON

Salmon have strong tails that help them leap up waterfalls.

SANDPIPER

Sandpipers fly in tight group formations, to avoid being singled out by predators.

SEAGULL

Seagulls can drink both freshwater and salt water.

SEA HORSE

Sea horses have no stomachs.

SEAL
To keep cool, seals flip sand on their backs when lying on a beach.

SEA TURTLE
Sea turtles travel thousands of miles in the ocean; females return to the beach where they were born to lay their eggs.

SHARK
Sharks are able to sleep while they swim.

SHEEP
Sheep can see behind themselves without turning their heads.

SKUNK
Skunks do not like the smell of their own scent.

SLOTH
It takes a sloth one minute to move twelve feet.

SLUG
Slugs make slime that helps them slide over surfaces like grass or rock.

SNAIL
Snails are more active at night.

SQUID
One kind of squid has the largest eyes of any animal.

SQUIRREL
Squirrels can smell nuts that are underground, but they often forget where they buried their own nuts.

STARFISH
When a starfish loses an arm it will grow back.

SWALLOW
Swallows catch and eat insects while they are flying.

SWAN
Swans can hiss.

 SWORDFISH
Swordfish don't use their swords to spear prey, but use them like a club.

 TARANTULA
Some tarantulas produce silk from their feet.

 TICK
Ticks only eat three times in their lives.

 TIGER
Tiger cub eyes stay closed for the first ten days or so of their lives.

 TOAD
Toads blink when they swallow.

 TROUT
Trout have an excellent sense of hearing.

 TUNA
Tunas are fast swimmers, and can reach speeds of almost fifty miles per hour.

 TURKEY
The skin on a turkey's face and wattle changes color if it is irritated.

 TURTLE
Turtles have been on Earth for over two hundred million years.

 UAKARI
Uakaris' red faces become pale when they are sick.

 UMBRELLA BIRD
Umbrella birds have a wattle on their necks that helps amplify their call.

 UPUPA
The upupa is named after its call oop-oop-oop.

 URCHIN
Urchins have sharp teeth that can drill holes in rock.

 VAMPIRE BAT
Vampire bats not only fly, they also scoot along the ground.

VIPER
Vipers can stretch their mouths open to swallow prey three times their own bodies' width.

VOLE
Voles can give birth to a hundred babies in a year, because of large litters and a short gestation.

 VULTURE
Vultures poop and pee on their legs to keep themselves cool.

 WALRUS
Walruses use their tusks to break through ice.

 WARTHOG
When warthogs run they hold their tails straight up in the air.

 WASP
Some wasps can chew wood, making a papery material they use to build their nests.

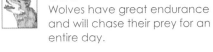 **WEASEL**
Weasels change the color of their coats with the season.

 WHALE
The humpback whale can sing continuously for twenty-four hours; their song can be heard over twenty miles away.

 WOLF
Wolves have great endurance and will chase their prey for an entire day.

 WOLVERINE
The jaws of the wolverine are so strong it can eat frozen meat.

WOMBAT
Wombats are mostly solitary, but sometimes visit other wombats in their burrows.

 XERUS
Xeruses hold their tails over their heads to shade themselves from the sun.

YABBY
A yabby's shell will match the color of the water it grew up in.

 YAK
Yaks use their horns to shovel snow and get at plants underneath.

YAPOK
Yapoks have both webbed feet and stomach pouches.

 **YELLOW JACKET**
A yellow jacket's stinger has small barbs.

ZEBRA
Zebras often stand with their heads resting on another zebra's shoulders, allowing them to see predators coming from both directions.

 ZEBRA DOVE
Zebra doves bow at each other when courting.

 ZEBRA FINCH
Young zebra finch males imitate the song of their father and will sing that song for life.

 ZEBRA FISH
Zebra fish are see-through.

 ZEBU
Zebu have large flaps of skin under their chins called dewlaps.

WHAT ELSE?

There are 8 hummingbirds on the front of the book jacket. There are 8 mice on the case under the jacket, along with 1 of every other animal in the book. There are 26 animals on the title pages, 26 animals on the front endpapers, and 26 animals on the back endpapers (one for each letter of the alphabet). There are 184 different animals featured in the book in total.

AUTHOR'S NOTE

I consulted many excellent books in my research, especially *Zoology*, by Joëlle Jolivet; *The Animal Book*, by Steve Jenkins; *The Sibley Guide to Birds*, by David Allen Sibley; and the Smithsonian Institution's *Animal: The Definitive Visual Guide to the World's Wildlife*, edited by David Burnie and Don E. Wilson. I also spent a lot of time at the American Museum of Natural History.

My thanks to Dr. Sacha Spector, Director of Conservation Science at Scenic Hudson, for his animal guidance. Thanks to Paul Greenberg, Alexandra Horowitz, Rebecca Schosha, Janice Nimura, Barney Latimer, and Elise Cappella for some great animal facts. And special thanks to my daughters, Zoë and Mia.